I0830742

WHERE DEMONS HIDE

WHERE DEMONS HIDE

Written and Illustrated
by Julianne Stone

3,863 Miles

West

They were late. I probably shouldn't have been surprised. They were always late to everything, and usually I couldn't give a shit. Time moved slowly here, and I'd spent most of the past three years making sure no one really expected me to fill it with anything important. It wasn't their job to know that all of that had changed for me.

I silently willed each car that passed to turn into the parking lot as I stuffed my hands in my jacket pockets and leaned back against the cold metal post of a handicap parking sign. Florida autumns were temperamental, especially this late in November, and this overcast night was accompanied by a rare razor sharp breeze that blew out to the ocean behind me. It wasn't the coldest I'd ever been by far—I don't think Florida had it in it to produce that kind of freeze, but it still managed to bite at my fingers and ears the longer I stood there.

My numb fingers brushed over the pack of cigarettes in my pocket, and out of habit I pulled the pack out and flipped the top open. Surely lighting one of these babies would warm me up just a little bit, but after a long moment of staring them down I shook my head and stuffed them back in my pocket.

A car turned in to the parking lot and pulled in to the space in front of me. At least this one piece of my poorly constructed plan was falling into place, though this did nothing to ease the tightly wound tension in my body.

Lucas stepped out of the driver's side and Vince, ever Lucas's shadow, emerged a moment later from the passenger side. The car was nothing fancy. It was an old sedan, its sand-colored paint dull and rusting away, its headlights foggy. But it ran and that's all that really mattered.

"Westley!" Lucas greeted me with a hard smack on the back. "My favorite customer! How are you doing tonight? Sorry to hear about Simon, man. That whole situation was real tragic. He was a good guy."

I don't think Lucas ever really meant what he said. He'd always had a silver tongue, ever since I met him three years ago in high school. I was a sophomore when he and Vince were seniors, and they were the only people who would talk to me that year. Turned out they were nice to everyone they thought they could sell some weed to and I was the kind of person who would buy weed from someone just for the company.

"Thanks," I said, not fully sure what I was thanking him for. I pulled a roll of money from my back pocket and started to count out what I owed him for the car.

"Whoa, look at money bags over here," Lucas said. "Why are you carrying around so much cash, man?"

"This is literally all I've got," I said, pulling out a little more than half and holding it out to him. I shoved the rest in my pocket as he took it and began to count it himself.

"Are you skipping town?" Vince looked at the two duffle bags and guitar case at my feet with narrowed eyes.

"Just going on a road trip," I said.

"You still owe me," Lucas said as he pocketed the cash, "a lot more than this."

"I'll pay you when I get back, man. You know I'm good for it."

"No, West, you'll pay me now. Whatever you've got. I'm not letting you skip outta here until I've got that money in my hand."

"I need this for gas and food," I said. "I won't make it past

Georgia without it."

"Tough shit. You heard what he…" Vince's voice trailed off mid-sentence as his gaze drifted over my shoulder and a confused look washed over his face.

I turned to look out at the beach. In the dark of the moonless night, I could just make out the silhouette of a girl running down the beach. Her movements were clumsy and haphazard, and as we watched she tripped and took a few more stumbled steps before collapsing into the sand.

"What the—" Lucas said under his breath.

Thankful for the distraction, I peeled away from the two and took off through the dunes and out onto the sand. The girl was slowly pushing herself up to her knees, and I noticed she was holding her left arm close to her body. Strands of her long, blond hair hung over her face as she looked up at me with wide eyes and then glanced behind her.

"Please help me," she said. "They're coming."

I looked up to see what she was looking at. Down the beach I could just make out two dark figures sprinting through the sand. One of them shouted something, but his words were carried out to the ocean by the wind.

I turned back to the girl. "Come on," I said, grabbing her right arm and putting it around my shoulders. Her skin felt ice cold to the touch, and all she had on was a tank top and some gym shorts. Blood stained her shirt near her left shoulder. A white scar in the shape of an X stretched across her left cheek. It traveled from the corner of her eye to her bottom lip and from the bridge of her nose to the angle of her jaw.

My first thought was that she must have been brave to wear a piece of her history on her face like that, but of course she didn't choose to have that scar. None of us chose to be damaged, we just were.

Together we made our way back towards the car. She kept glancing back at the two figures. They were gaining fast.

Lucas and Vince just watched. "Is she okay?" Vince asked as I pushed past him and led her to the passenger side of the car. "What's going on?"

"I don't know, man," I said, "but we gotta get out of here."

I wrenched open the door and helped her into the seat. As I stood back up and turned to head to the driver's side, Lucas moved to stand in front of me, and a moment later Vince slunk around him to do the same, trapping me against the car.

"I told you," Lucas said, his voice low and menacing, "you're not going anywhere until I get my money."

I wanted to tell him that we could talk about it later, to get in the damn car with us for all I cared, that we had far bigger fish to fry than a few hundred bucks of unpaid weed money, but before I had a chance to say any of that, he grabbed my shirt and threw me to the ground. Vince swung his leg back and landed a solid kick to my stomach, knocking the air from my lungs.

Lucas pulled out a pocket knife and flipped it open. "Now, are you going to give it to me, or am I going to have to take it fro—"

Before he could finish his sentence something… impossible happened. As if they were hit by an invisible truck, Lucas and Vince flew off of their feet and were flung ten yards to my right, landing hard on the asphalt in the middle of the parking lot. They lay motionless for a few moments before I heard one of them moan and the other let out a string of expletives.

I turned my gaze back to the car where the girl now

stood, leaning heavily on the open passenger side door, her left arm outstretched. It was my first time really getting a good look at the arm, and I wasn't sure how I possibly could have missed it before. From just below her shoulder all the way to the tips of her fingers, her arm was made entirely of an onyx colored metal, and between the seams in the joints it glowed a bright blue, as did the irises of her eyes.

She turned to me and her intense expression softened. Her eyes then went to her arm, and she stared at it like she'd never seen it before either. The glow in the arm and her eyes faded and she slumped back into the car, her gaze now distant.

I scrambled to my feet, blood rushing through my ears as I slammed her door shut and then sprinted around to the other side of the car, scooping up my bags and guitar case as I went. I tossed them in the back seat and slid into the front. The key was still in the ignition—thanks, Lucas—and as soon as the car roared to life I peeled out of the parking spot and made for the exit.

As I turned on to the main road, I was able to catch just a glance in the rear view mirror of the two dark figures from the beach slowing to a stop next to Lucas and Vince as the boys pushed themselves to their feet.

"What the hell was that?" I said, my knuckles white around the steering wheel. "Who were those people? Who are *you*?"

"I-I don't know," she said. She sounded like she was in shock.

"Which part?"

"All of it. I can't remember… anything."

I cursed and gripped the steering wheel so tight that my knuckles turned white. Adrenaline was still pumping through my veins and I had no idea what to do. I didn't need this. I didn't need any of this.

"I think you just ran a red light," she said.

"God damn it." The last thing I needed was to get pulled over. I turned the car into the parking lot of a restaurant, its spots all empty this time of night, and rolled the car to a stop. I closed my eyes and took a moment to breathe, to calm myself and my racing mind, to restrain myself from lighting the entire pack of cigarettes in my pocket and smoking them all until I couldn't breathe anymore.

"You don't have anywhere to go, do you? Someone I can call?"

She shook her head.

I couldn't leave her here to fend for herself, I knew that for sure. The cops would have more questions for me than I could ever hope to answer, and every comic book and movie on the planet told me that handing her over to the law would only lead to bad things for her. It was a dumb thought, but the logic seemed solid. People hated things they didn't understand, and what I'd just seen her do was pretty unbelievable.

"I'm skipping town," I said after a long silence. "Tonight. Right now. And I'm never coming back." I looked over at her, and she was staring at me, her light blue eyes wide. "Do you want to come with me?"

She nodded.

I smiled, hoping she couldn't see the storm of uncertainty that was brewing inside of me. "My name is West," I said, holding out my hand.

She took it with her normal, flesh-and-bone hand, and though she was freezing and exhausted and probably scared out of her mind, she smiled too. "I'm Coral."

2,716 Miles

Coral

My eyes flew open and I sat up, shards of panic stabbing at me from every side. For a second I couldn't remember where I was—my mind was still foggy and it was hard to find the right thoughts through the haze, but after a moment I recognized the interior of the car and the brown leather jacket that was now draped over me.

I let my body relax and collected my memories. There weren't many. They felt choppy and disjointed, but each one stuck in my mind in different ways. There was the cold metal of the table against my back. The sound of my bare feet slapping against concrete floors. The sweet, salty smell of the ocean. The electricity that coursed through my veins as those two men flew through the air at my command. And his smile. West's warm, welcoming smile.

The car sat parked outside a squat white gas station, and West's seat behind the wheel was empty, but all of his things were still in the back. Half a dozen empty soda and energy drink cans littered the dash board. I had fallen asleep soon after we had pulled onto the highway, but it looked like West had driven straight through the night.

I grabbed one of the cans, setting it upright at the edge of the dash. I sat back as far I could in the seat and raised my left arm. My shoulder ached every time I moved it, and the skin where the metal met flesh felt raw, but I needed to test it. I needed to make sure what happened the night before wasn't just some fever dream.

I focused, letting the feeling of sparking electricity course through my veins again. It was so much easier than I thought it was going to be. I just had to think about what I wanted to happen, and it did. The arm lit up that icy blue color again. The can slowly lifted a few inches off of the dash and stayed suspended in mid-air, leisurely rotating in place.

I let my arm drop into my lap and the can fell with a clink onto the plastic of the dash, bouncing off to land at my feet. The glow faded after a few seconds, but the electricity lingered.

The driver's side door suddenly opened, making me jump. West—his dark, curly hair peeking out from under a baseball cap that was pulled low over his eyes—plopped down in the seat, tossed the empty cans that were in the cup holders up onto the dash, and replaced them with fresh ones.

"Morning, sunshine," he said. "You slept like a rock. And

for like 16 hours, too. I'm impressed. The longest I've done is like 13 or 14, I think."

"I did?" I said. I still felt exhausted. "Where are we?"

"Just outside of Dallas."

I searched my memory for a Dallas. It was frustrating having so many holes in my mind. I knew that I should know things, like where I grew up or the name of my 5th grade teacher or where the hell Dallas was, but when I went to the spot in my brain where those things should have been, I came back empty.

West must have seen this internal struggle on my face because he leaned over to the glove compartment and pulled out a map. He unfolded it and spread it out over the dash so we could both see it.

"We started here," he said, pointing to a dot on the map that was labeled *Cocoa Beach*. He slid his finger up along the coast, then over to the left and landed on another point. "And now, we're all the way over here in Dallas, Texas. Fifteen minutes outside of it, really."

"And where are we going?" My eyes danced over the map, from name to name, hungry for all of this wonderful new information.

West slid his finger all the way to the top left of the map. "Seattle, Washington," he said. "I grew up there with my mom. I'm going back to see her."

"That's lovely," I said.

"I can drop you off wherever you want, though, as long as it's not too far off the path."

I shook my head. "I don't really have anywhere to go."

"Well, then you can stick with me 'til we get there," he said. "Seattle is a great city."

He handed me the map and then turned around in his seat and began rummaging through his bags in the back. A few moments later he emerged with a pair of jeans, a black t-shirt, and some thick boots. "Here, and keep the jacket, too. It's pretty cold out."

I took the clothes and handed the map back to him. As I did I noticed his eyes linger on my metal arm.

I quickly slipped the shirt and pants over the clothes I was already wearing. They were both a little too big, but they'd work for now. The jacket was soft and warm and still smelled like the ocean. It covered up most of the metal arm, too, just leaving my hand visible.

"Thanks," West said, "for what you did for me last night. I just... you really saved my ass." His gaze met my eyes for only a moment as he fidgeted in his seat.

"You saved me, too," I reminded him.

"Yeah," he said. He shook his head. "Hey, are you hungry? I saw a diner across the street."

"I'm starving," I said. "I can't remember the last time I ate."

West smiled and he shot me a sideways look. "Was that a joke?"

I smiled and shrugged.

He laughed. "You really are something, Coral." He handed me the neatly refolded map. "Why don't you hang on to this? I marked the route we're taking so you can look at it whenever you want and figure out where we are."

I took it and slipped it into the inside pocket of the jacket before pushing open the car door and stepping out into the fresh air of the early evening. The sun hung just above the orange trees as I followed

West across the street to a small building that glowed with long tubes of blue and pink neon lights. The inside was buzzing with conversation and the clattering of silverware against plates. A smiling waitress greeted us as we walked in and led us to an empty booth near the back. We sat across from each other, and the waitress set two menus in front of us before wandering away. We looked over the menus in silence. I read each item carefully, but nothing really stood out to me as something I remembered liking, so when the waitress came back with drinks, I just ordered the same as West.

"So, Coral, you gotta help me out a little because it's all I've been able to think about the entire time you were sleeping, and it's driving me crazy. How the hell did you fling Lucas and Vince clear across the parking lot last night?" West said.

"How many times are

15

you going to make me tell you that I don't know?" I said. "I can't remember anything."

"But you remember some things," he said. "I mean, you know your name."

"I know what a hamburger is, too, but I don't know if I like it. I know what a map is, but I couldn't remember what any cities were called. Things are spotty. Everything from my past before last night is just a big black void. I've been trying so hard to remember, to figure out what happened last night, just like you, but I just can't." I looked down at my hands resting on the table. One whispered of a secret history through chipped nail polish and freckles that dotted the skin like stars in the night sky, and the other was sleek and cold and totally silent.

"Alright, alright. Why don't you tell me what you *do* remember? Then maybe I can help you piece some of it together, get some answers for both of us."

I closed my eyes and directed everything I had towards remembering every detail of the night before. "I woke up on a table," I said. For a moment I could feel the cold metal against my skin and it sent a shiver down my spine. "I was in the middle of a large room with huge, round lamps hanging from the ceiling, and these weird machines pushed against the wall, but it was dark and really quiet. The only light was coming from the hall, so I got up and I went out there. The ground was cold and hard, I think concrete? From down the hall, I heard a man yell… I don't remember exactly what he said, but whatever it was it was enough to tell me that I had to get out of there… so I ran. I followed the exit signs to a big metal door, and then I ran across a long stretch of grass, and then I was out on the beach and, well, you were there for the rest."

"There were two people chasing you," West said.

"Yes. There was a woman there too, but she didn't say anything."

"Shit," I heard West breathe.

I opened my eyes. He was looking at something over my shoulder, and as I twisted around to look at the wall-mounted TV tuned in to the evening news, I was greeted with a familiar face. My own. I looked younger in the picture, my hair shorter and glowing gold in the sunlight. Beside it the name "Coral Leon" was written in bold white letters.

It was kind of comforting to know that I could recognize my own face, but I didn't remember the photo having ever been taken, and there was something in it I didn't recognize. My hand went to my cheek and absently traced over the X-shaped scar to confirm that it was truly there.

I could just hear what the news anchor was saying over

the din of the diner. "—has been missing since late last night. She was last seen in Cocoa Beach, Florida in a tan sedan with an unidentified Hispanic man in his late teens or early twenties. They are both wanted for questioning for the murder of two men—" the images of Lucas and Vince replaced my face on the screen "—though the police have not disclosed their involvement in the deaths. If you have any information, please call the number on your screen—"

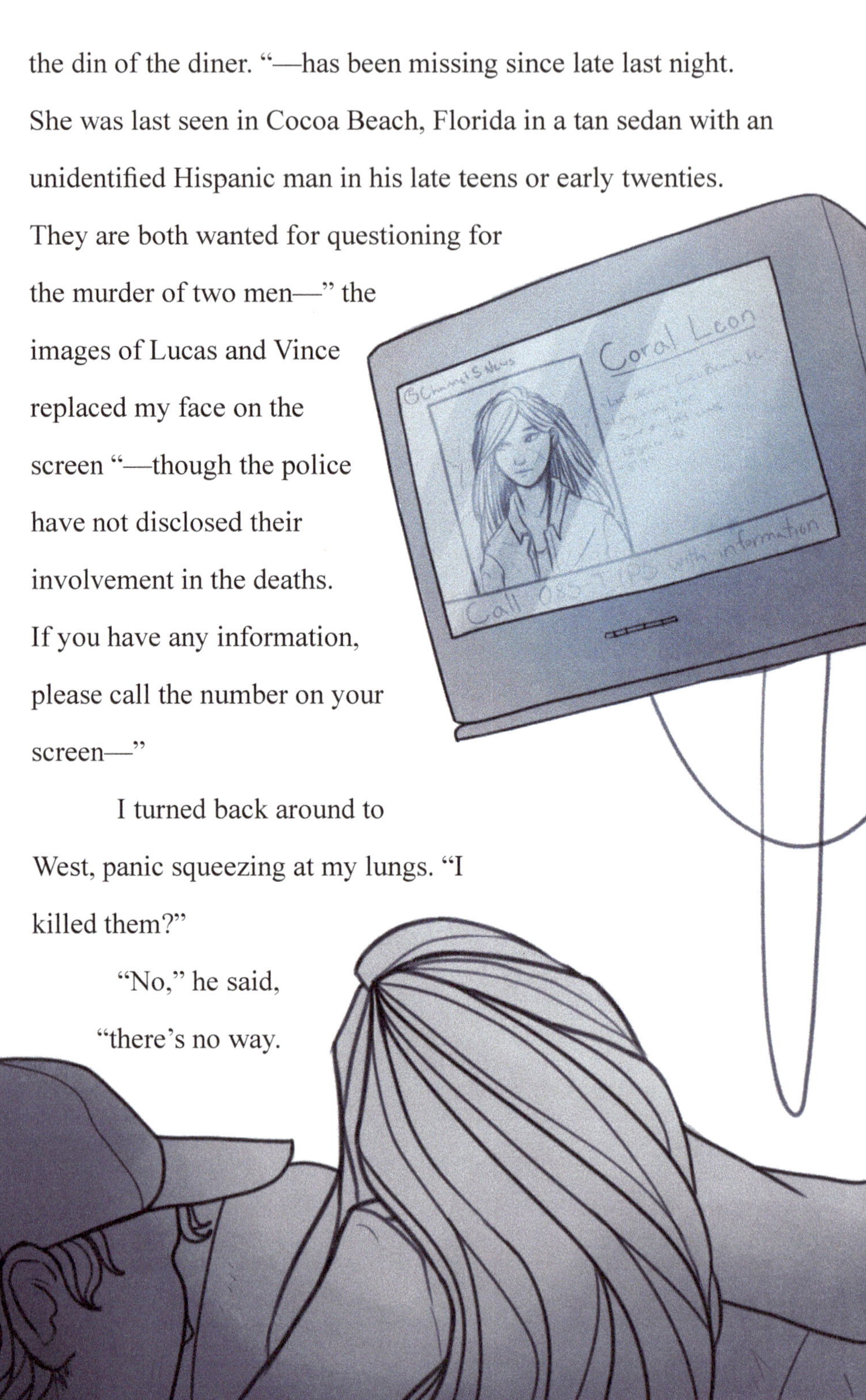

I turned back around to West, panic squeezing at my lungs. "I killed them?"

"No," he said, "there's no way.

They were alive when we left. I saw them get up. The most you did was give them some cuts and bruises." He sounded sure of this, but that still didn't ease the ball of anxiety building in my chest.

I scanned the room to see if anyone had noticed the news story, and at first it seemed like we were in the clear, but then I noticed our waitress on the other side of the diner. She was looking directly at me as she was talked apprehensively into the phone at the register. When she noticed us staring at her, she gasped and quickly turned her back to us.

West must have noticed her as well, because when I turned back to him he was already placing some money on the table and sliding out of the booth. "Come on, follow me."

Instead of going to the front entrance, West led the way into the kitchen. It smelled overwhelmingly of grease and meat and sweat. The man flipping burgers narrowed his eyes at us and turned to stand in the slim pathway between the stove and the bubbling fryers. "Hey you two aren't supposed to be back here."

"Good, we were just leaving," West said. He grabbed my hand and pushed past the fry cook, almost sending him back onto the stove top.

We flew out the back door and sprinted across the street. In no time at all, we were in the car, pulling out of the gas station parking lot, and racing down the road.

2,395 Miles

West

I wanted to put as much distance between us and that diner as I could, but as darkness settled in around us and the hours dragged on, I realized that I was fading fast. I hadn't slept in over a day and a half, hadn't eaten a real meal since the evening before, and all the energy drinks were doing now was putting me on edge and filling my bladder.

Coral had been looking at the map for a while as the sun was setting, but now that it was dark she just sat quietly, watching as fields and cows and trees passed by. I was sure she hadn't killed Lucas and Vince. They were still alive when we left, but I didn't know how to make her believe that.

I pulled off the highway and rolled the car to a stop on the side of a dirt road in Middle-of-Nowhere, Texas. The car fell eerily quiet as I turned off the engine and sat back into my seat.

"I was thinking," Coral said after a long stretch of silence, "you keep asking me all these things that I don't have the answers to, but you haven't really told me about yourself." She was playing with the corners of the folded up map, almost pointedly not looking at me. "Why are you helping me? Just being near me is dangerous. I'm dangerous. There's nothing in this for you."

I stared at her for a long moment at a loss for words. "Coral…" I said. "Come with me." I pushed open the door and stepped out of the car, grabbing my guitar case from the back seat as I went. Coral just sat and watched me with her eyebrows furrowed. "Come *on*! I'm going to tell you about myself and someone much more important than me, but we're not going to do it in that stuffy car on a night as beautiful as this one."

I swung the door closed and hoisted myself up onto the roof of the car. I set to work tuning the guitar as Coral took her time getting out of the car, climbing up on the hood, and then finally settling down beside me. The moon drifted above us high in the sky, and out here so far from any cities or towns, the sky was bursting with bright, twinkling stars. Coral stared up at them as my fingers danced over the strings of the guitar, her mouth slightly open. I wished I could have known what she was thinking in that moment, because I'm sure it was something just as beautiful as the sky above us.

"When I moved to Florida," I said, my fingers still strumming away at the guitar, "I was pretty much alone for a long time. I knew a few people, and we spent time together because we were useful to each other, but I didn't really have anyone real until I met Simon. We had the same math class junior year. It was a class I had no business being in, you know? I guess there was some scheduling mix-up or something because everyone in that class was so smart and, well… let's just leave it at I *really* shouldn't have been in that class. But if it hadn't been for that mistake, Simon and I would have never met."

Coral's gaze drifted away from the sky and turned to me. She pulled her knees to her chest and wrapped her arms around her legs as she listened to my story.

"He helped me through the class and we became really close. We started a band with two of his buddies. I sang and played the guitar and he played the drums, and we were *good*, man. Like, we could have made it somewhere. Simon and I wrote all the songs together. We poured out all of our problems and worries and everything into these songs and eventually, I realized that I loved him in a way that I had never loved anyone before.

"And then last November he was diagnosed with brain cancer. The really, really bad kind. It was like the universe had realized it had fucked up and the burnout stoner kid wasn't supposed to end up with the bright, kind, selfless one in this story. It picked the wrong one to get rid of to fix it."

I swallowed hard, trying to push away the tears that were building behind my eyes. "It was rough near the end. He started to forget a lot of things. We would sing our songs together to pass time at the hospital and he would forget the words half way though. He'd tell me that he just wanted to listen to me sing, but I could see the frustration in his face.

"He died on Monday. His funeral was last night. His mom wouldn't let me in the church. I guess she'd read his texts or something and found out about us. She didn't want me there reminding her that her son wasn't the perfect, mindless drone that she wanted him to be. And I guess she'd called my dad and told him everything as well because when I got home he called me every homophobic slur in the book and told me I had twenty minutes to get out of his house. So I packed up everything that mattered—which turned out not to be much—and I left."

I stopped playing and let the music of the night—the distant chirp of crickets and the breeze dancing through the grass and the clicks and creaks of the car as it cooled below us—fill the air instead. "And with all of the money to my name, I bought a shitty car and I drove across the country with a lost girl. Between us, we brought a lot of demons along for the ride. And it wasn't easy, and sometimes it was scary, but we were a pair of freaks and she was actually pretty funny when she wanted to be, so we made it work."

A sad smile danced over her lips. "I'm sorry about Simon," she said. "He sounded like a wonderful person."

"He was. He was one of the best." I smiled as a wave of memories washed over me. "He was weirdly obsessed with the meanings of people's names. His means 'listen,' which I think fits really well. My full name, Westley, means 'some guy who lives in that meadow over there,' which is kinda bullshit, but he always thought it was really funny."

"What does mine mean?" Coral said.

"Well, your first name is just the sea plant thing, right? But your last name… holy shit."

"What?"

I thought I had recognized Coral's last name, Leon, when I saw it on the TV in the diner, but at the time I didn't really have a second to think about it. But now, as I thought about its meaning, a memory suddenly popped to the front of my mind.

I set the guitar aside and pulled my phone from my back pocket, furiously tapping away as I talked. "I've spent a lot of time at the hospital in the past few months, and spending that much time just sitting around with nothing to do, even an idiot like me will pick up on a few things." I turned the phone around so that she could see the website that I'd pulled up with logo of a roaring lion at the top. "Leon. They're a prosthetics company with insanely revolutionary tech. There was a girl at the hospital who lost her leg in a car accident. She was a track star at her college and she was sure she would never run again and lose her scholarships and everything. She ended up getting an amazingly cool prosthetic one from Leon and it was insane how fast she recovered. She back to her old self in weeks."

Coral took the phone from me and began scrolling through the website. I watched as her scrolling grew faster and faster. "These kinda look like my arm," she said. She suddenly stopped scrolling and her whole body went tense. "That's them," she almost whispered, as if she would get in trouble if she said it too loud. "Those were the people I saw last night."

I took the phone back from her and examined the picture. On the left was a middle-aged man with a full head of dark hair that was just starting to go gray. His face was narrow like Coral's, but the rest of her features were reflected in the woman to the right side of the photo. She had long blond hair and blue eyes, but her gaze was much colder than Coral's. Where Coral's eyes were a cloudless summer sky, this woman's were razor sharp shards of ice.

"Martin and Angela Leon," I read just below the photo, "co-founders of Leon Cybernetic Solutions. Martin is an award-winning biologist, and Angela is a world renowned engineer, according to this."

I spent the next few minutes Googling a few things, but besides some articles about their work and a TED Talk Martin gave in 2013 about how nerve endings work or some shit, I came up empty. "I can't find anywhere that says they have a daughter, but… there's no denying you look just like them."

Coral was staring out at the endless flat fields that disappeared into the darkness around us, but I could tell that she wasn't looking at anything in particular.

"When I saw them," she said, "my gut instinct was to run, to get as far away from them as I possibly could." Her gaze shifted to me, her eyes earnest and intense with what I could have sworn was a slight blue glow. "They aren't good people. I feel it in every bit of my body that is still mine. They are evil."

1,533 Miles

Coral

We spent a long time on the roof of the car that night staring up at the stars, both of us quietly stewing in our own misfortune. After a while West decided to get some sleep and slid off the roof of the car to return to the warm interior. I stayed out for a while longer, but eventually I followed suit and fell asleep in the back seat.

We woke the next morning with the sun as it rose above the distant tree line, and West was soon back behind the wheel. He still looked exhausted, but when I offered to drive and he asked me if I even remembered how to drive, he didn't seem satisfied with my answer of, "Well, we can find out."

We only stopped for gas and to get drive-through burgers every few hours, not wanting to risk repeating the ordeal at the diner. Turned out I did, in fact, like burgers, and after full day without food, I couldn't get enough of them.

"What's with that stupid grin on your face?" I said around

hour seven of driving.

"I just had an idea," West said.

"Yeah? Do you want to share?"

"Nah, I think I'll keep it a surprise."

Whenever we passed a city as we drove, West would call out the name and I'd find it on the map. Cities and towns were pretty few and far between as we exited Texas, sped across New Mexico, and made our way through Arizona. Between them, I made West tell me about places he'd been and then tried to find them on the map as well. These were harder to find since they weren't ones along the route, but that was half the fun, and the stories that went with them were all so interesting. I noticed all of the ones in Florida were about Simon, about the places their band had played or weekends they just

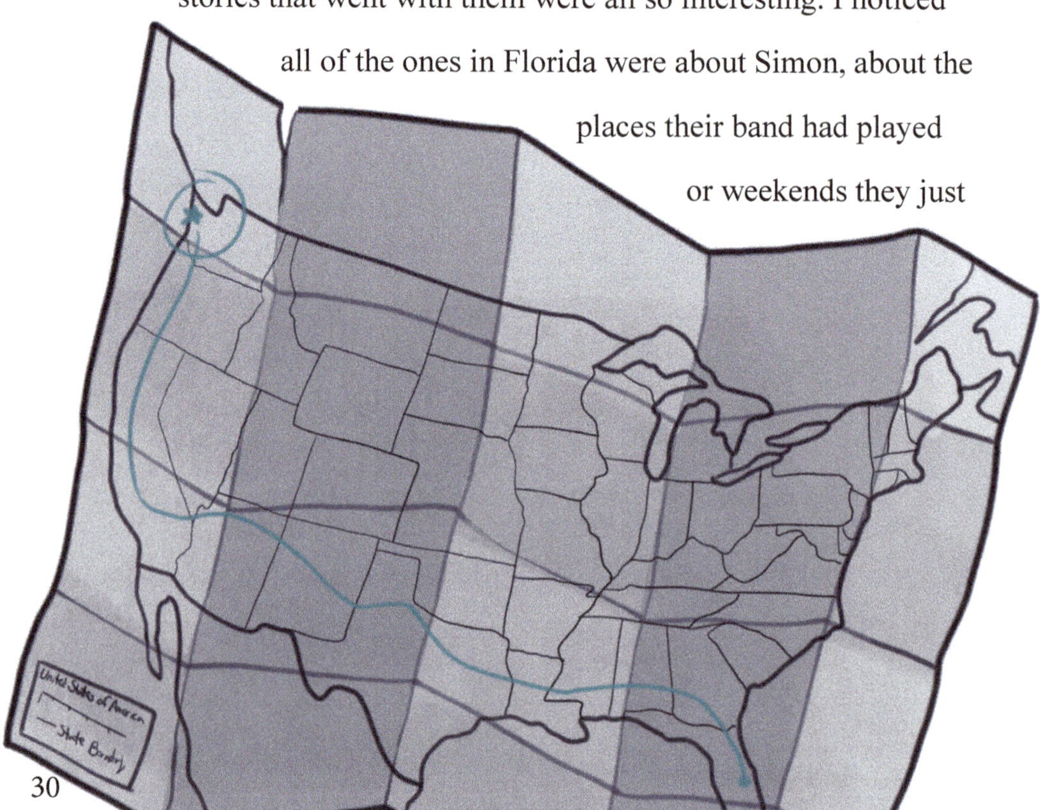

spent getting away from their families.

"Hey, put away the map," West said.

"What? Why?"

He shot me a mischievous smile. "We're coming up on the surprise soon and I don't want you to figure it out before we get there."

I narrowed my eyes at him and smiled as well. "Or, I could just look to see what we're near real quick. It would be *sooo* easy."

He laughed. "Come on, just go with me here. It'll be so worth it."

"Fine," I said, folding up the map and setting it in my lap. "Happy?"

"Ecstatic."

We pulled off the highway and drove down some lightly trafficked two-lane roads for a while. It was so different here than way back where we started. Everything was hills and sand and wiry little trees that looked like a slight breeze would lift them right out of the dusty soil. The air was so dry, too. It was a wonder anything could survive in a place like this.

West pulled the car to a stop at the back of a line a few cars deep at a building that looked like a rustic, deep-woods toll booth.

"I'll be honest, this is not what I was expecting," West said, mostly to himself. "I thought you could just drive up to it…"

We crept slowly forward with the line, and as we pulled up to the booth, a bored-looking, twenty-something guy slid open the window. "Welcome to the Grand Canyon," he said in flat tone without looking up. "One day parking is $30."

"Shit," West grumbled, pulling his quickly shrinking roll of cash out of his pocket and handing over two twenty-dollar bills.

He paused for just a moment to look at us as he took the money. "One second while I get your change," he said, and then quickly slid the window closed, disappearing into the booth.

"Grand Canyon?" I said.

"I've always wanted to come here," West said. "It's a little out of the way, but I figured why not? How often are we going to have freedom like this, to just go wherever we want without anyone caring or needing us to be somewhere else? So fuck it, right? Though thirty bucks… we might be a little tight for cash by the end of this trip, but I think we can make it work."

"But what's so special about this place?"

"You just have to see it." He turned back to the window. "What the hell is taking this guy so long?" He reached out and rapped his knuckle against the glass a few times.

A moment later the booth attendant reappeared and slid open the window. "Sorry about the delay here's your change have a nice day," he said in one breath before almost throwing the ten-dollar bill at West and sliding the window shut again.

West stared at the booth bewildered for a moment before shoving the money in his pocket and directing the car forward down a narrow, twisting road.

"Close your eyes," he said. "I think we're almost there."

"What?"

"You're killing me, Coral. Just humor me."

"Fine, fine." I closed my eyes.

We continued on for another minute before I felt the car stop and he turned off the engine. "Stay there," he said before I heard his car door open and close. A moment later my door opened and I felt West's hand on my right arm. "Follow me. And keep your eyes closed!"

I blindly stepped out of the car, and he looped his arm around my elbow.

"Alright, we're in a parking lot, so I'm gonna try really hard to not get you hit by a car," he said.

"I'd very much appreciate that, thanks," I laughed.

"Step up here. There's a curb."

"Shit."

"Watch it, don't trip."

"Literally the only thing I can't do right now is 'watch it,' West."

"Bad wording, I admit it. But, here, just put out your arm and there should be a railing there."

I heard a *tink* of metal against wood as my left hand made contact with the railing and I gripped it tight.

"Alright," West said. "You can open your eyes."

The whole earth seemed to drop off in front of me and open up to a beautiful, strange, breathtaking world of orange and yellow stone that stretched on as far as I could see. I leaned over the railing to see that past the jagged rocks and steep walls, a tiny

river of blue snaked its way through the floor of the canyon. It was terrifying and it made me feel so small, but that's what drew me in and made it so I never wanted to look away.

West leaned against the railing and the biggest, dumbest smile spread across his face.

"Yeah, this is so much better than seeing it on a screen."

"It's pretty amazing," I said.

West stepped up on one of

the lower lateral rungs of the railing and hoisted himself up so he was two or three feet off the ground with his knees resting against the top of it.

"What are you doing?" I said, instinctively grabbing on to his pants so he wouldn't pitch forward into the canyon.

"Therapy," he said before throwing his head back and yelling at the top of his lungs. No words, just pure, unfiltered emotion.

I glanced around at the other people around us, who were all looking up at West, some with bemused smiles on their faces and others just confused and a little bit scared.

"Alright, West," I said, tapping his leg, "come on, people are staring. Get down."

He looked down at me. "Come on, you've got to try it. Just once, then I'll get down."

"Are you serious?"

"I mean, you're a badass with super powers, you can do—or not do—whatever the hell you want, and I'm really in no position to stop you. But I can tell you it feels really good. So hell yes, I'm serious. Go for it!"

I glanced around at the other people again. Some were still watching us, but most had gone back to looking out at the canyon or had wandered away. I sighed. "Fine."

I leaned into the railing, gripped it tight with both hands, closed my eyes, and let out a long, guttural scream. I didn't hold anything back. I let all of the fear and frustration and dread that had been stirring inside fuel me. West was right. It felt really, really good. I felt free, like I was floating on air. Like nothing mattered in that moment.

I felt a hand pull at my arm and West's frantic words of, "Shit, Coral, stop," and I opened my eyes. My boots dangled a few feet off the ground as a dozen or so rocks drifted and danced through the air around me. It felt like the air itself was keeping me aloft. I felt another tug on my jacket. He wanted me to come down, but this felt so amazing. I felt so truly free, and he was just trying to chain me back to the earth. A spark of annoyance danced over my skin and down my arm.

Leave me alone. The thought was so sudden and harsh that it didn't feel like it was my own. Suddenly, West flew away from me, stumbling backwards a few steps like I had pressed both of my hands against his chest and shoved as hard as I could. My breath caught in my throat and the soles of my shoes slapped against the pavement as I returned to reality. A barrage of orange stones plummeted to the earth a moment later. I looked down at my hand just as the bright blue glow started to fade away.

"West, I'm so sor—"

"Don't worry about it," he said, his gaze flicking around the crowd of tourists around us.

People were definitely staring now. I could feel their fear and confusion burning holes in my skin. I backed away from the railing a few steps, and then turned and headed out towards the parking lot. West was close behind me, and soon took the lead weaving between parked cars. Eventually I spotted the safe haven that was West's car, but there was a woman standing behind it. She was very official looking in a tailored suit and with her hair pulled into a tight bun. She was writing something in a note pad and slowly circling the car.

"Wait," I said, catching his arm and pulling us both behind a dark SUV. I silently pointed in the direction of his car. He peeked out from behind the SUV and let out a string of quiet curses as he spotted the woman, too.

"Okay, you stay here. I'll go see what her deal is," he said. He stepped out into the open and strode over to his car with confidence in his step. "Hey, can I help you?"

"Is this your car?" She said.

"Yeah, why are you hanging around it?"

"I'm Special Agent Jane Thompson from the FBI," She said, pulling something from her pocket and quickly showing it to him. He was taller than she was, and she didn't seem more than five or six years older than us, but in that moment he seemed to shrink to the size of a child.

"You're FBI? Like *the* FBI?"

"Yes sir, just like that. What was your name?"

"Uh, West. Westley Wallis."

"Are you traveling alone, Westley?"

"I am," he said. He was taking slow steps towards the driver's side door.

"Have you seen this girl before?" She pulled a picture from the front of her note pad, and West leaned in to look at it.

His shoulders tensed, but he kept his voice even as he said,

"Nope, never seen her before."

"Are you sure? Look closely. She has a distinctive, X-shaped scar on her cheek. She's been missing—"

"Look lady, I'd really like to help you, but I'm meeting up with a friend soon and I'm already late, so if you could just…"

"Of course," she said, stepping out of the way of the car.

"You know, there were some weirdos screaming out at the canyon a little bit ago, maybe you should go investigate that instead of bothering random people," West said before ducking into the car.

She watched as he backed out of the spot and drove down the aisle, turning at the end and disappearing behind the row of larger cars. She sighed, stored her notepad and pen in her pocket and pulled out a phone and a set of keys. The SUV beside me chirped and the door I was leaning against suddenly unlocked. Panic suddenly surged through me as she turned and started heading in my direction.

On instinct, I lifted my left hand, focused on one of the cars behind her, and let off a blast of energy. My hand lit up and that familiar electricity coursed through my body as the car jolted. Its headlights started flashing and an alarm screamed at full, earsplitting volume. She jumped at the sudden commotion and turned to see what it was, and I took that moment to slip away from her car and run as fast as I could down the next aisle while keeping my head low. West was waiting at the end, and when he spotted me he stepped on the gas, stopping just barely long enough for me to hop in and close the door before we were speeding away.

1,406 Miles

West

I hated Las Vegas. Everything felt so artificial. The buildings, the people, the atmosphere; they were so over the top that it all just felt so obviously, desperately fake. I would have avoided the city entirely if not for one of my former bandmates, Tess, who'd moved out there a year ago with the standing offer of free beer and a safe couch to sleep on. After Coral losing control at the edge of the canyon and our encounter with the FBI agent, a safe place was exactly what we needed.

Though our destination was on the edge of the city, I made sure to drive down the strip for Coral. I mean, I really did it so I could see Coral's reaction, which was totally worth it. Her eyes were the size of dinner plates the entire time as she alternated between looking out her window and leaning over me so she could look out of mine. She kept excitedly pointing out weird-looking buildings and extravagantly dressed people, but I just watched her. She was the most genuine person I'd met in a long, long time, and watching her in all of her excitement—the neon lights of the strip turning her skin bright pink and her eyes an ethereal purple—was strangely healing.

I was completely exhausted by the time we made it to Tess's apartment, which was on the top floor of an old, renovated industrial building. After pounding on the door for a solid ten minutes and calling her cell three times with no answer, I leaned back against the door defeated, dreading having to get back in the car and stay conscious long enough to find another place to stay. The past few days of barely any sleep were starting to catch up to me.

"Maybe I can unlock it from here," Coral said. "Your friend wouldn't mind, right?"

"She said I could come by whenever," I shrugged. "Go for it."

Coral placed her left hand over the lock and closed her eyes. There was a flash of blue and a loud metallic *crunch* and her eyes flew back open, surprised. "I don't think that worked the way I wanted it to."

I twisted the knob and the door moved about half an inch before catching. Taking a moment to brace myself, I threw all of my weight into the door with my shoulder. It sprang free and I stumbled into the apartment. The deadbolt fell at Coral's feet in three mangled pieces.

"How did you manage to do that?" I said.

Coral crouched down and picked them up. "I have no clue."

The apartment was huge and sparsely furnished. It was all one room, not counting the bathroom. There was a small kitchen, a couch sat in front of a TV, and up a few stairs there was just a mattress with some blankets and a pillow haphazardly tossed on top.

I grabbed my bags from the hall and tossed them beside the couch. "Tess?" I called out to the empty apartment. "You're not here, right?"

Coral closed the door behind us and gingerly set the pieces of the shattered dead bolt on the counter.

"Seems like the coast is clear," I said. "She's probably out of town or something. I think she joined a new band a while back that's doing pretty good."

"She doesn't have much stuff."

"Yeah, I think she became a minimalist or something? I don't know, she was always kinda weird."

We settled down on the couch and I flipped on the TV. I spent the next half hour trying to explain what was happening in an episode of Breaking Bad until, without really meaning to, I drifted to off sleep.

I dreamt I was at the Grand Canyon. I had my toes on the edge and strong wind at my back, and I was losing my balance. Just as I was about to fall, someone caught my wrist. I looked around to see Coral. Her eyes were that icy, glowing blue and her expression was filled with rage and disgust. Her metal arm gripped my wrist so hard it felt like it was going to break.

And then, she let go. I was falling. The bottom of the canyon rushed towards me at dizzying speeds, and at the bottom, calmly staring up at me, was Simon.

Just before I crashed into him, I woke up.

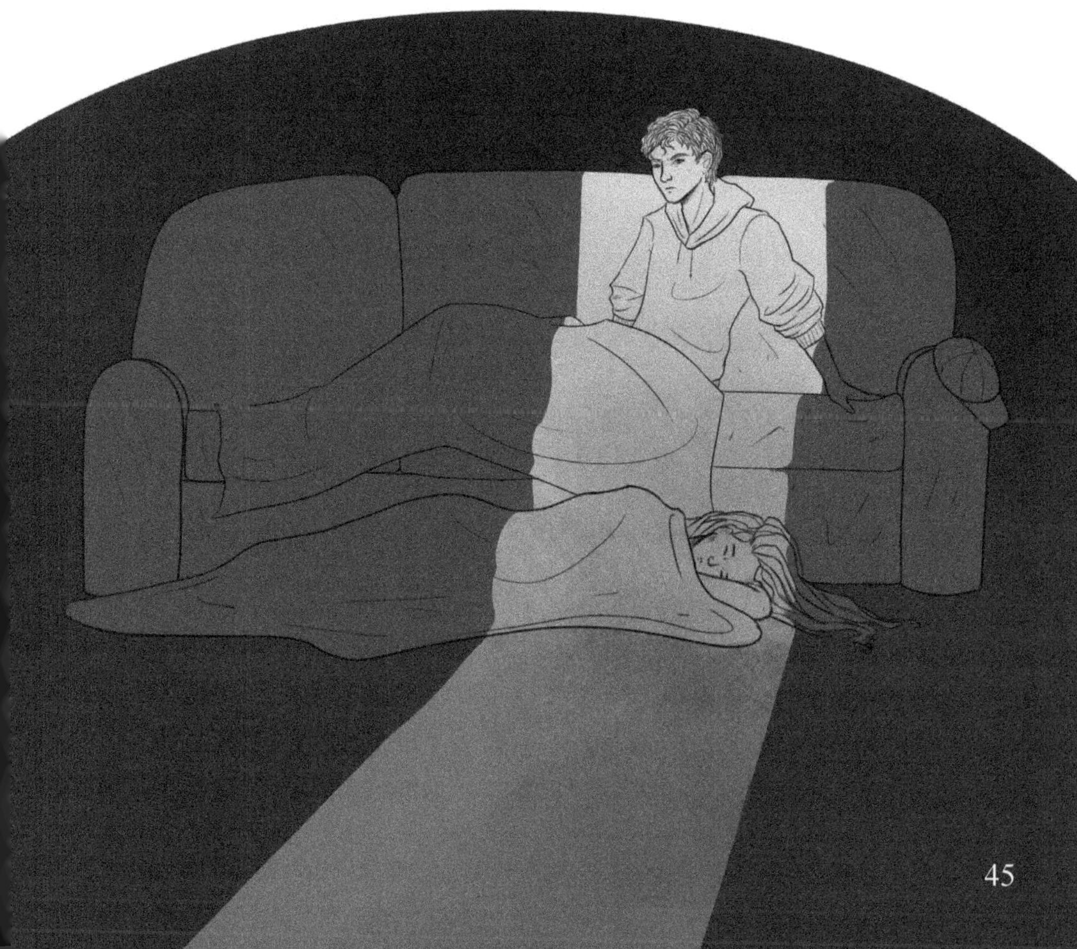

The front door to the apartment stood wide open. The light from the hall was just bright enough for me make out Coral's sleeping form on the floor. I slowly got to my feet, making sure not to step on her.

"Tess?" I whispered. "It's me, West. Sorry we broke in, I couldn't get a hold of—" My breath caught in my lungs as I turned to find a gun pointed directly at my face.

"Don't move. FBI."

I slowly put up my hands and stared down the gun at Agent Thompson.

"I thought you said you didn't know her," she said.

"Oh *this* was the girl you were looking for? Well shoot, if you'd have just told me that I would have been happy to hand her over to you. I'm sure she'd be thrilled to hear that she'll be going back to her pair of comic-book-villain parents."

"Her parents have a right—"

"They don't have a right to *anything* that has to do with her anymore. Have you even taken three seconds to Google her? She didn't exist to the rest of the world before two nights ago. Those psychos don't care about her safety. They just want her back so they can keep doing whatever they did to her before that fucked up her memory."

She lowered the gun slightly. "What are you talking

about?"

"They didn't tell you that, did they? There's a hell of a lot more where that came from. The Leons are not good people, and if you take her back to them they are going to make sure she disappears again, this time to a place she'll never come back from."

Agent Thompson sighed. "Westley, I was just assigned the case this afternoon because I was the closest to the Grand Canyon. I read the file. Maybe what you're saying is true, but I can't just let you two go. I still have to bring both of you in. It's my job."

Coral suddenly sat up and blue light filled the room. The agent lifted off her feet and flew backwards and slammed against the wall before crumpling to the floor.

Coral's hands went to her mouth and she stared at the agent with horrified eyes. "I didn't mean to do it that hard," she said, scrambling to her feet. She pushed past me and dropped to her knees in front of Thompson. She rested her hand on Thompson's chest over her heart and then let out a sigh of relief. "She's still alive."

"How did she find us?" I said, joining Coral beside Thompson's unconscious body.

"No clue…"

I searched her coat pockets and produced her note pad, her

wallet, and a familiar folded up piece of paper.

"The map?" Coral took it from me. "I must have dropped it at the canyon. I'm so sorry."

"Don't be," I said. "I shouldn't have brought us there in the first place. It was stupid."

"But it was beautiful."

"Yeah… it was…"

My gaze went back to the agent. This was the third time in the last twelve hours that Coral had lost control of her powers. I felt like I knew her pretty well already, and I knew that she would never hurt someone intentionally, but it was starting to seem more and more like it wasn't always up to her.

"We need to go before she wakes up," I said. "Would you do me a favor and take my bags down to the car? I'm going to write Tess a note to apologize for the lock."

"Yeah," she said distantly. "Okay."

She numbly got to her feet, collected the bags, and disappeared down the hall.

I waited for the door to the stair well to slam shut at the end of the hall before opening Agent Thompson's wallet and pocketing one of her business cards.

"Just in case," I said to myself. "It's just a last resort."

With guilt settling down heavy on my shoulders, I put all of her things back in their respective pockets and followed Coral outside.

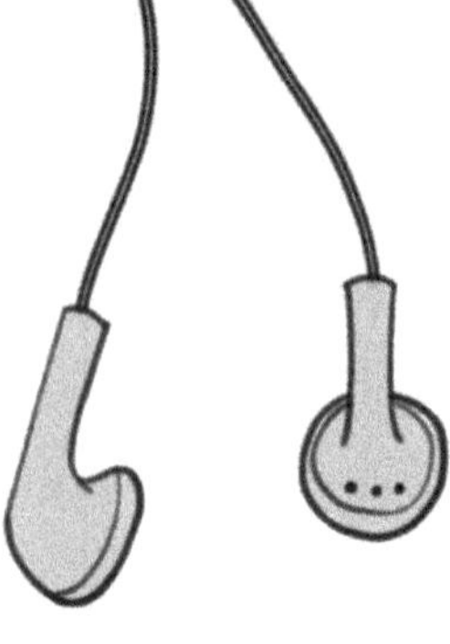

752 Miles

Coral

I slept most of the way through Nevada. When we hit California and turned north, the sun was just starting to peek over the horizon, I took to staring out the window. West still told me which cities we were passing and when the next one would be coming up. I tried to act like I was interested, but I kept the map closed and hidden inside my jacket pocket. I was tired, physically and emotionally. I was tired of not remembering and I was tired of feeling so out of control. I could tell his heart wasn't in it either. He'd been acting strange since we left the apartment. Eventually we just fell into silence.

West pulled off the highway around Sacramento and stopped outside of a bakery. His car door opening almost before the key was out of the ignition. "I need *so* much coffee right now, and if I don't walk around for a bit I'm gonna lose my mind. You should probably stay here. Do you want anything?"

"I'm okay, thanks."

He gave me a sad smile. "We're in the home stretch now. We just have to get through today, okay? By dinner we'll be in Seattle eating some supremely better burgers than what we've been living on."

"That sounds great."

He stepped out of the car and closed the door behind him, leaving me to relish in the silence of the dormant car for a minute. The constant hum of the engine was starting to drive me a bit crazy. It felt like the white noise was fueling my spiraling thoughts, but this peace was enough to calm my mind just a little.

Something buzzed in the center console beside me, the sudden noise startling me. I pushed aside some empty chip bags to reveal West's phone sticking out of the cup holder. I picked it up and pressed the button on the front, and it lit up to a lock screen. Under the time and the date, a text message from his dad stared impatiently up at me.

Your face has been all over the news, it read. *What the fuck did you do? Call me!*

At the bottom of the screen, in little flashing letters, it said, *Press home to open.* So I did. I was immediately met with the faces of Martin and Angela Leon. I guess West had left up the web page that we'd been looking at two nights before, or he'd been looking at it recently. Either way, the little digital eyes of my parents were staring up at me now. They were the only people on the planet who truly knew who I was, and the thought of that filled me with dread.

I skimmed the bio under the photo, but it was basically just a long-winded version of what West had told me about them the other night. Underneath it, though, there was a phone number in blue text.

I hesitated for a long moment, my thumb hovering over the number. *They could have answers,* I told myself. *They might be able to fix you.*

I took a deep breath and pressed my thumb against the glass. The screen changed and I could faintly hear the dial tone coming from the speaker at the top, so I pressed it to my face and waited.

"Martin Leon's office, how can I help you?" It was a woman's voice, too chipper for me.

"I'd like to speak to Martin," I said, trying to sound like I meant it.

"Sure, do you have an appointment?"

"Um, no. Just tell him that it's Coral. Please, it's important."

"Sure thing, just hang on the line one second for me."

Some jazzy music started paying over the speaker and I sat back against the seat, my stomach churning like the ocean in the middle of a hurricane. I tried to rehearse what I was going to say to him, but it all sounded so dumb and childish.

Suddenly, too soon, the music cut off.

"Coral?" It was a man's voice this time.

"Is this Martin?"

"Coral, where are you?" It was hard to read the emotion in his voice. He sounded very professional, but also there was urgency in it. I couldn't tell if it was worry or impatience.

"We're in California," I said.

"California? How the hell did you get all the way out there? Coral, you should be in one of our facilities right now under observation. We don't know how you could react to the implants."

I clenched my metal fist. "So you did do this to me."

"Do you not remember?"

"I can't remember *anything*, Martin. Like, at all."

"Interesting," he said quietly, mostly to himself. "I thought

that could have been a possibility, but the initial brain scans didn't
indicate anything went wrong…"

"Are you kidding me?"

"Coral, I think I know what happened. The implant we put
in your head so that your brain can communicate with the arm is
interfering with your hippocampus, the place where your memories
are stored."

"So how do I fix it?"

"We have the equipment here that should fix it in a few
minutes."

I fell silent, my mind racing. "I'm not going back there."
Everything inside of me recoiled at the idea.

"Coral, think about it. Would you rather live your entire life
on the run, lost, alone, and confused, or do you want to come home
to your family where it's safe and we can take care of you?"

"I just want my memory back," I said, "and I want to stay
with West."

"Well, you can't have it both ways."

I closed my eyes. I wanted to scream and cry and demand
that he give back to me what was rightfully mine, but I knew that
would somehow make this all worse. I loved West. He was my
lifeline. But without my memories I felt empty, like the shell of
a person who lived her life and earned her scars and then left me

behind to fend for myself.

"We'll be in Seattle in twelve hours," I said softly. "Can I meet you there?"

"I'll get on a plane right away," he said. "You're making the right choice here."

He gave me an address where I could meet him when I got there, which I quickly wrote in the corner of the map, and I hung up the phone.

27 Miles

West

"Is something wrong?"

We were almost to Seattle. I could barely hold in my excitement, but it seemed like the closer we got to the city, the more Coral shrank into herself.

"I'm fine," she said softly.

"Are you feeling okay? If you're hungry, I think there's still a bag of chips in the—"

"I'm not hungry." She sat up. As she ran her fingers through her hair, I noticed that her hand was shaking. She pulled the map from her pocket and put it on the dashboard between us. "I need you to drop me off at the address written on there."

"What? I thought you and I were—"

"West, please," she cut me off again. "This is important to me."

"*What* is important to you? What's going on?" My palms suddenly felt very sweaty against the steering wheel. "Look, I know I said at the beginning that we'd split once we got here, but we can stick together for as long as you want, okay?"

She shook her head. "I want to, I really do, but there's other stuff I have to do first." She looked like she was about to cry.

"Coral…" I said, suddenly connecting the dots in my head. "Tell me you're not going back to those Leon Cybernetics assholes."

"I called my dad," she said. "He said he could get my memories back really easily. I know they're bad people, but they help people too. They gave that girl her legs back. And I escaped from them once, right? With what I know I can do now, how hard could it be to do again?"

"They're not *just* bad people. They're also geniuses. Those two things don't mix well." I shook my head, trying to wrap my brain around this while also keeping my attention on the road. "I'll go with you. My thing can wait."

"No. I don't want to put you in danger, too," she said. "I'll be fine. I'll find you after it's all over."

"You're not giving me a choice here, huh?"

"No, I'm not."

I sighed and shook my head, turning my full attention back to the road. She sat back against her seat and we continued on in icy silence.

The tall glass skyscrapers of the city soon rose up around us, reaching towards an overcast sky. We rolled over rainbow colored sidewalks and past wall after wall covered in murals and street art. The sidewalks outside of bars were already crawling with patrons, and I could just imagine the vibe inside with a band up on the stage and a hundred voices singing along with them. This city was my favorite place on earth, but today, somewhere within it there was darkness, and I was driving straight for it.

The address led us to a warehouse near the bay. There was no sign outside, just the street number painted in huge letters over the door. I pulled the car up to the curb and turned off the engine.

"Are you sure you don't want me to go with you?" I said.

"I'm sure," she said. She picked up the map off of the dashboard. "Do you mind if I take this?"

"It's yours." I swallowed hard, trying to keep my voice steady. "Hey, if I don't see you again…thank you. For everything."

Coral threw her arms around me, burying her face in my shoulder. I squeezed her tight. I wanted more than anything to never have let go, but eventually she pulled away, wiped the tears from her cheeks, and left the car without another word. As I watched her walk away I pulled a cigarette out of my pocket, lit it up, and took a long drag.

As soon as the door of the warehouse swung closed

behind her, I got out of my car, dropped my cigarette in the street, and headed towards the building. I walked past the front door and around to the side alley, pulling out my phone and Agent Thompson's business card.

"This is Westley Wallis," I said as soon as she picked up. "I need your help. Coral is in danger. Her psycho of a father somehow convinced her that her only option was to go back to him. I think he's going to hurt her."

"Westley? Where are you?"

"In Seattle. You followed us here, right? There's no way you didn't make a copy of that map." I gave her the address of the warehouse. "Please, you have to believe me. Martin and Angela Leon are dangerous, and Coral just walked straight into their den."

"I know they are. I did some research on the plane ride here, and you were right. Coral has no birth certificate, and she has never been enrolled in school or been to the doctor. I've also found dozens of reports of malpractice during clinical trials at LCS that have just been swept under the rug," she said. "I'm on my way."

"Great, I'll be inside."

"Wait, Westley, no! Stay out—"

I hung up the phone before she could finish and rounded the corner to the back of the building. I tested the knob to the back door, which was mercifully unlocked. I took just a moment to open up the voice memos app on my phone and hit record before pulling the door open and heading inside.

It took a few moments for my eyes to adjust to the darkness. Slowly, towering shelves came into view, all filled with Plexiglas boxes containing various prosthetic body parts. I knew they were all fake, that most of them would be going to people who really needed them, but that didn't stop it from looking like the inside of a serial killer's trophy room.

"What do you mean? You said on the phone that you knew how to do it!"

It was Coral's voice, and she definitely did not sound

happy. I crept down the row of shelves and peaked around the last box. Coral stood about twenty feet away with her back to me. With her were two faces I recognized. Martin and Angela Leon.

Angela took a step forward to put a comforting hand on Coral's arm, but Coral shrugged it off.

"We don't think it's in our best interest anymore," Martin said. "You didn't tell me the whole truth about the side effects when we talked earlier. I had to learn about your episode at the Grand Canyon from a YouTube video." The venom in his voice was so potent that even I felt the need to shrink away from him. "What that arm can do, it surpasses anything we thought possible. We can't risk messing up the conditions that made it possible until we understand how it works."

"You were never going to fix my brain, were you?" Coral said.

"I have some theories on what happened there," he said, "but right now that is on the bottom of my list of priorities."

"You *liar*!"

Coral's hand suddenly lit up like a Christmas tree. Angela gasped at the sight, but Martin remained stoic. He tucked his arms behind his back and looked down his nose at Coral.

"I'm not going with you anywhere." She threw off her jacket, revealing the entire arm, the blue light swirling with pure energy within. "You never cared about me. I don't need my memory to know that for a fact. You never cared about her either." She jabbed her finger at Angela, who flinched. Coral's feet lifted off of the ground and the shelves around her started to rattle like she was the epicenter of an earthquake. "You don't care about anyone but yourself."

As calm as ever, Martin pulled a gun from behind his back and pointed it directly at Coral. "There's only two ways you're leaving here today, Coral. An autopsy won't be as useful to us as a live subject, but at least it would be something. It's your choice."

Her golden hair whipped around her like a steady wind had just picked up in the middle of the warehouse. "Fuck you."

Martin's face suddenly twisted in anger. I saw his finger tense over the trigger and, without a second

thought, I sprang from my hiding place and launched myself in their direction. Angela was the fastest of all of us, though. As quick as a fox, she darted forward and slapped a small, metal disc on the wrist of Coral's metal arm. For a moment, I thought—or hoped, really—that it did nothing, but then arcs of white electricity curled up her arm. She seized for a moment, her movements sporadic and jerky, before she crumpled to the ground.

I screamed, just like we did out at the edge of the Grand Canyon, but now the grief and pain that I'd put into it the first time was accompanied by pure rage. Martin turned the gun to me, and a sudden, ear-splitting *BANG* echoed across the building. My shoulder was suddenly consumed in piercing, blinding pain.

I dropped to my knees next to Coral.

Martin took a few steps forward and aimed the gun at my forehead. "Westley Wallis," he said, "so nice of you to join us. It's a shame you and your friends back in Florida had to get caught up in all this, but you have to understand, I can't have anyone else getting a hold of my work. I have to tie up loose ends."

I closed my eyes. I was sure that this was it, that in a second I would have a bullet in my brain and that Coral would be carried off to some facility to be tested on for the rest of her life.

And then I heard the four most magical words I would ever hear in my life.

"FBI! Drop your weapon!"

0 Miles

Coral

West was waiting for me outside the police station. He leaned against his rusty old car, his right arm in a sling and a hard cast, his left holding a bouquet of beautiful flowers, and his face sporting the biggest, dumbest grin I'd seen on it to date.

"All set?" he said.

"Just gave my last statement, at least for now," I said. "Are you ready to go?"

"As ready as I'll ever be." He pushed himself off the car with a grunt. "It's only a few blocks away."

It was an unusually beautiful December day. The air still had a nip to it, but the sunlight on my skin more than made up for it.

"Are you getting used to not having the arm?" West said.

"Starting to." I rubbed my shoulder. Whatever Angela had done to me had fried all the hardware inside the arm, leaving it completely useless. It was weird sometimes when I forgot it wasn't there and tried to use it, but overall I felt lighter without it. I didn't have to worry about losing control anymore. I could start to be normal.

I hadn't remembered anything from my life before that night on the beach, and the doctors said that they weren't sure I ever would. After weeks of tests and scans and psychological evaluations, they couldn't figure out what Martin did to my brain. I was starting to think it was better this way. I didn't have to remember what he'd done to me for all of those years. My memory was just full of starry nights on top of cars and sweet music and the Grand Canyon and beautiful flashing neon streets.

"What are we going to do when the trial and everything is all over?" I said.

West shrugged. "We could start a band."

"Is music the only thing you can ever think about?"

"I think we could pull it off! Between the two of us, we have just enough arms to play a guitar right now. Can you sing? I can teach you to sing."

We turned into the graveyard and West led me down the path to a huge oak tree with a small, neat gravestone under it. The oak was bare of its leaves, but I could imagine it in the middle of summer, beautiful and green and swaying in the wind.

West set the flowers down in front of the grave stone.

"Hey, Mom," he said. "Sorry it's been so long since I visited. Three years… it feels like it's been longer. I have quite the story to tell you this time. It starts out sad, and it gets a lot sadder, but there's still hope and love and lots of adventure. There's a happy ending, too. I know you can't stand stories that don't have happy endings. Plus I have someone pretty amazing here to help me tell it. So…here it is..."

Thank you to everyone who backed
this book on Kickstarter. This little
book woldn't exist without you, and I am
forever grateful for your support.

Thanks to Mary, my original partner in writing crime,
for sticking with me and Coral from the beginning.

Thanks to Ath, Seshi, AJ, and Cosmo for being my
crack team of beta-readers and sanity-checkers.

Thanks to Michelle, just for everything.

And most of all, thanks to my parents for encouraging
me in all of my crazy dreams and for putting up with
me never letting them read my stories.
I hope you liked this one.